HOPSCOTCH FAIRY TALES

The Frog Prince

Retold by Anne Walter

Illustrated by Flory Denis

FRANKLIN WATTS
LONDON•SYDNEY

First published in 2009 by
Franklin Watts
338 Euston Road
London
NW1 3BH

Franklin Watts Australia
Level 17/207 Kent Street
Sydney
NSW 2000

Text © Anne Walter 2009
Illustrations © Flory Denis 2009

A CIP catalogue record for this book is available
from the British Library.

ISBN 978 0 7496 8540 9 (hbk)
ISBN 978 0 7496 8546 1 (pbk)

Series Editor: Melanie Palmer
Series Advisor: Dr Barrie Wade
Series Designer: Peter Scoulding

Printed in China

Franklin Watts is a division of
Hachette Children's Books,
an Hachette UK company.
www.hachette.co.uk

Once upon a time, a young
princess lived in a beautiful palace.

She loved to play with her golden ball in the palace gardens.

She could throw it high into
the air ...

but she hardly ever caught it!

One day, she threw her ball up, up, up. It sailed into the air … then straight down into a well!

"Oh no!" said the princess.
"My lovely ball! How will I get
it back?" She started to cry.

"Please stop crying, princess.
I can't stand crying!" croaked a
little voice. It came from inside
the well, so the princess peered in.

Deep down inside the well she saw a slimy frog. "I will get your ball," he said, "but only if you give me something in return."

"Anything!" promised the princess.
"Let me come and stay in your
palace," the frog said.

"I promise," said the princess,
thinking that the frog was joking.

So the frog fetched the ball and
threw it up to the princess.

She skipped away, bouncing
the ball all the way back
to the palace.

Next day, the king, the queen and
the princess were eating dinner
when there was a tap, tap, tap
at the door.

As the king opened the door, the frog leapt in. "I've come to stay, just as the princess promised!" said the frog, making himself at home.

"You can't!" said the princess.

"You should always keep your

promises," said the king,

"so the frog must stay."

The frog hopped up to the dinner table. "That looks tasty," he said. So the princess held out her plate for the frog.

He gulped and slurped and then
he burped. The princess wasn't
hungry anymore.

At last it was time for bed.
The princess opened the
door to let the frog out.

But the frog was already hopping
up the stairs, hippity, hippity hop.

The frog quickly leapt onto the princess's bed. "Mmm, so soft," he said, yawning.

"That's my bed!" said the princess.
But she knew she had to keep
her promise, so she had to share
her bed with the frog.

For weeks the princess shared
everything with the frog.

Then, one morning, the frog
had vanished.

"I'm still here, princess," said a voice. As the princess looked round she saw a handsome prince!

"A wicked witch put a spell on me, but by keeping your promise you have set me free," said the prince.

The prince asked the princess
to be his wife and took her
back to his wonderful kingdom
in the forest.

He took the golden ball, too, and
they lived happily ever after.

Put these pictures in the correct order.

Which event do you think is most important?

Now try writing the story in your own words!

Puzzle 2

1. I want to live in a palace.

2. I love playing games.

3. I order you to obey.

4. Never joke about making promises.

5. I don't like sharing things.

6. I'm good at jumping down wells.

Choose the correct speech bubbles for each character. Can you think of any others?

Turn over to find the answers.

Answers

Puzzle 1

The correct order is: 1d, 2e, 3f, 4a, 5c, 6b.

Puzzle 2

The frog: 1, 6

The king: 3, 4

The princess: 2, 5

Look out for more Hopscotch Fairy Tales:

The Emperor's New Clothes
ISBN 978 0 7496 7421 2

Cinderella
ISBN 978 0 7496 7417 5

Jack and the Beanstalk
ISBN 978 0 7496 7422 9

The Pied Piper of Hamelin
ISBN 978 0 7496 7419 9

Snow White
ISBN 978 0 7496 7418 2

The Three Billy Goats Gruff
ISBN 978 0 7496 7420 5

Hansel and Gretel
ISBN 978 0 7496 7904 0

Little Red Riding Hood
ISBN 978 0 7496 7907 1

Rapunzel
ISBN 978 0 7496 7906 4

Rumpelstiltskin
ISBN 978 0 7496 7908 8

The Three Little Pigs
ISBN 978 0 7496 7905 7

Goldilocks and the Three Bears
ISBN 978 0 7496 7903 3

For more Hopscotch books go to: www.franklinwatts.co.uk